THOMAS
& FRIENDS
Don't
Bother
Victor!
PETER SAM

Up in the hills above Sodor, Thomas met Peter Sam and The Thin Controller.

"I'm off to meet The Fat Controller today," said The Thin Controller. "So I'm putting you in charge for the day, Peter Sam!"

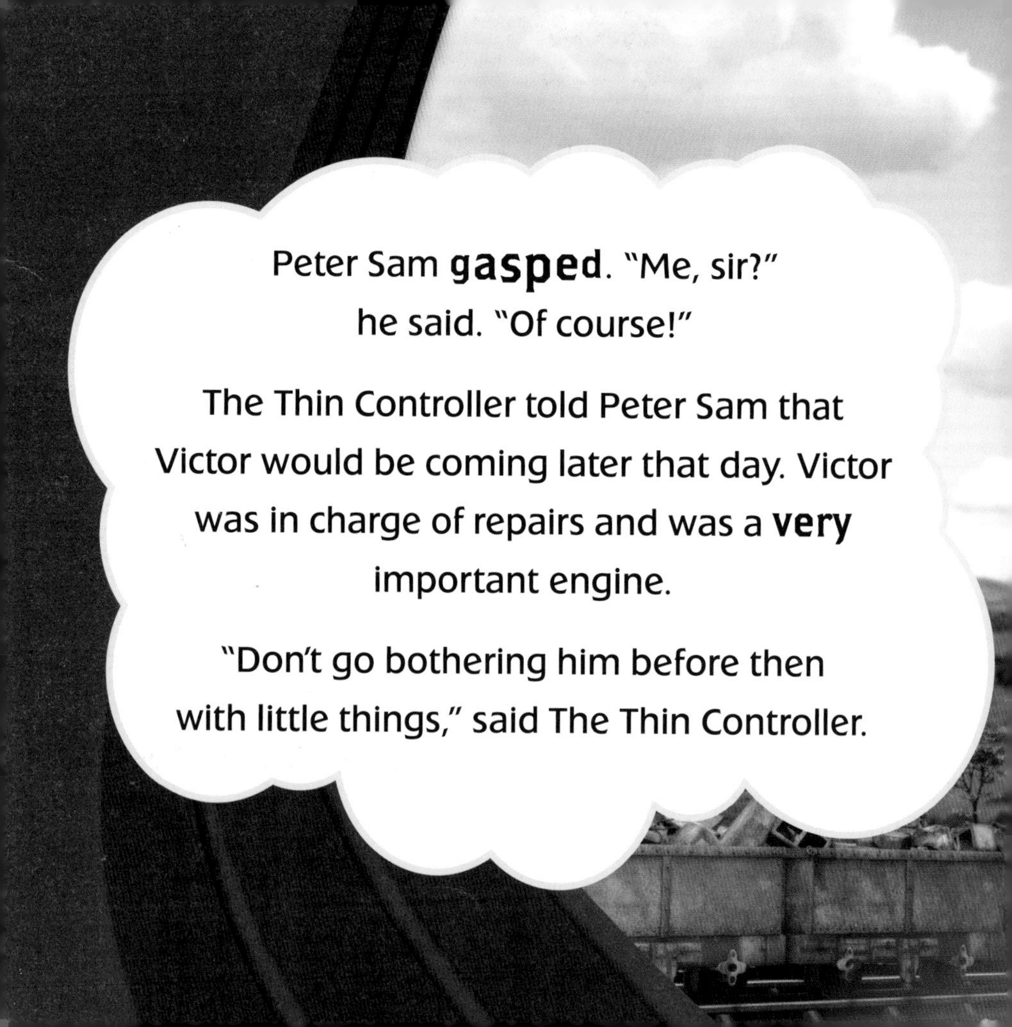

Peter Sam **gasped**. "Me, sir?" he said. "Of course!"

The Thin Controller told Peter Sam that Victor would be coming later that day. Victor was in charge of repairs and was a **very** important engine.

"Don't go bothering him before then with little things," said The Thin Controller.

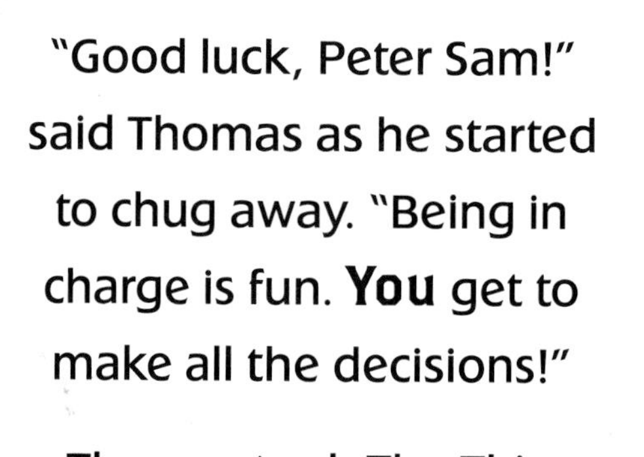

"Good luck, Peter Sam!" said Thomas as he started to chug away. "Being in charge is fun. **You** get to make all the decisions!"

Thomas took The Thin Controller to meet The Fat Controller. Peter Sam was left in charge.

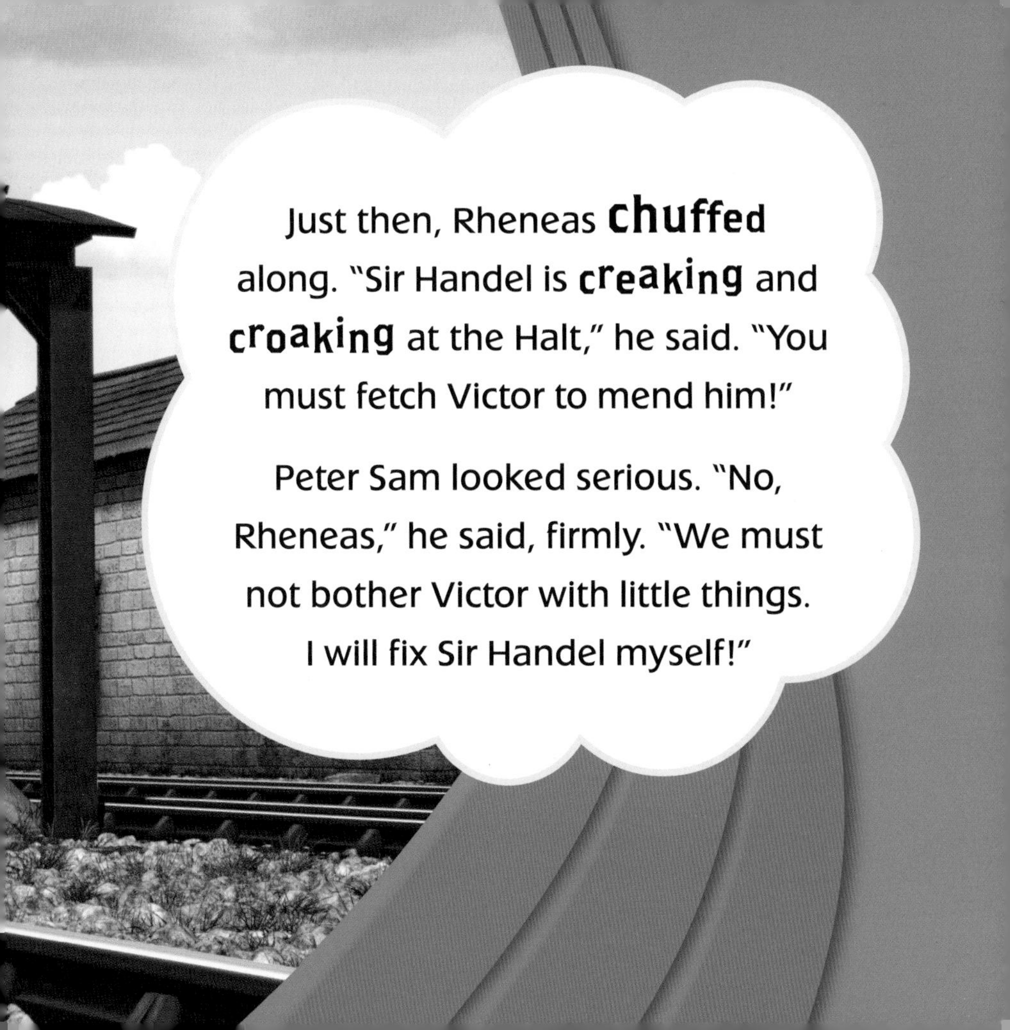

Just then, Rheneas **chuffed** along. "Sir Handel is **creaking** and **croaking** at the Halt," he said. "You must fetch Victor to mend him!"

Peter Sam looked serious. "No, Rheneas," he said, firmly. "We must not bother Victor with little things. I will fix Sir Handel myself!"

At Daisy Halt, Sir Handel was **creaking** and **croaking**. "Please fetch Victor!" he said.

"I'm sure I can fix you," said Peter Sam. "I think you need more oil."

So Sir Handel's Driver added more oil. But Sir Handel **creaked** more than ever!

Just then, Rheneas came along. "Now Skarloey's funnel is broken!" he said. "Peter Sam, you **must** fetch Victor!"

"We must ***not*** bother Victor!" said Peter Sam. "I will chuff to Skarloey and fix him myself." And off he puffed, leaving Sir Handel behind.

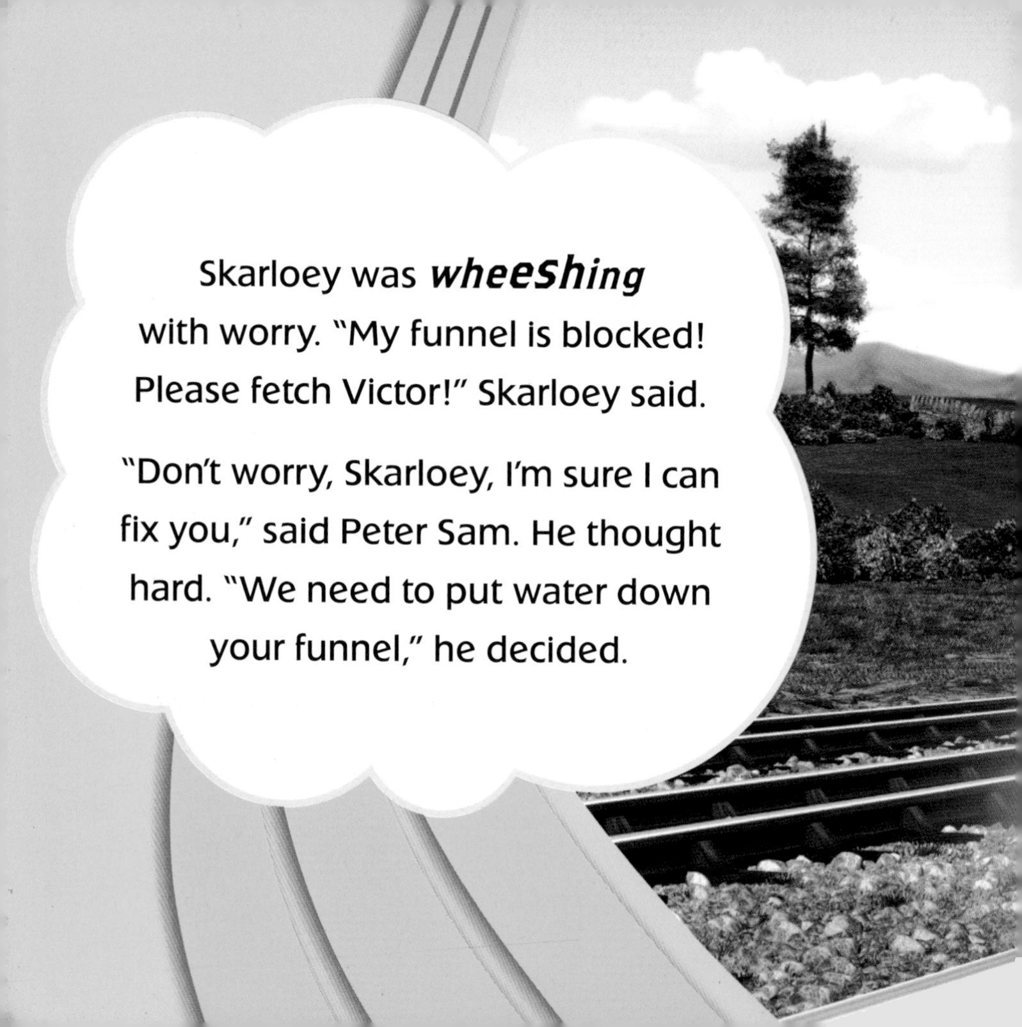

Skarloey was ***wheeshing*** with worry. "My funnel is blocked! Please fetch Victor!" Skarloey said.

"Don't worry, Skarloey, I'm sure I can fix you," said Peter Sam. He thought hard. "We need to put water down your funnel," he decided.

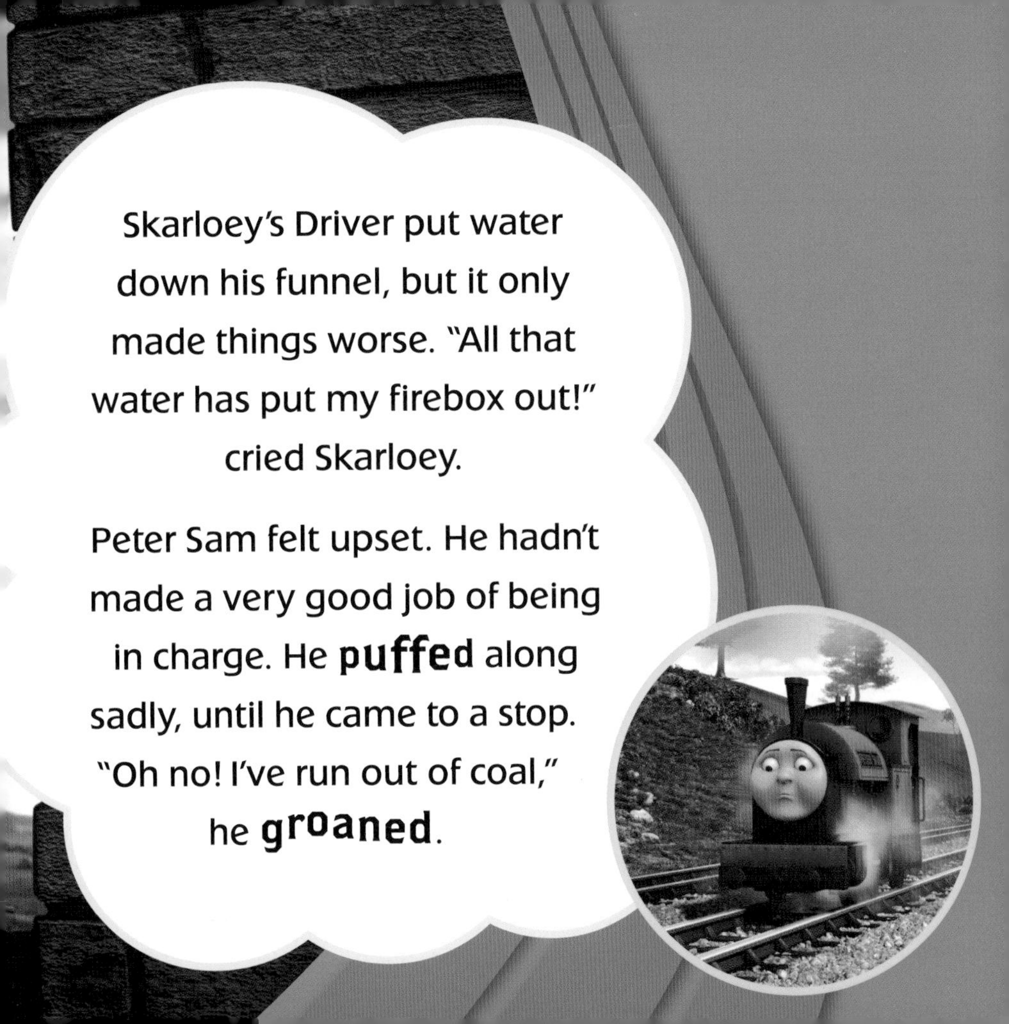

Skarloey's Driver put water down his funnel, but it only made things worse. "All that water has put my firebox out!" cried Skarloey.

Peter Sam felt upset. He hadn't made a very good job of being in charge. He **puffed** along sadly, until he came to a stop. "Oh no! I've run out of coal," he **groaned**.

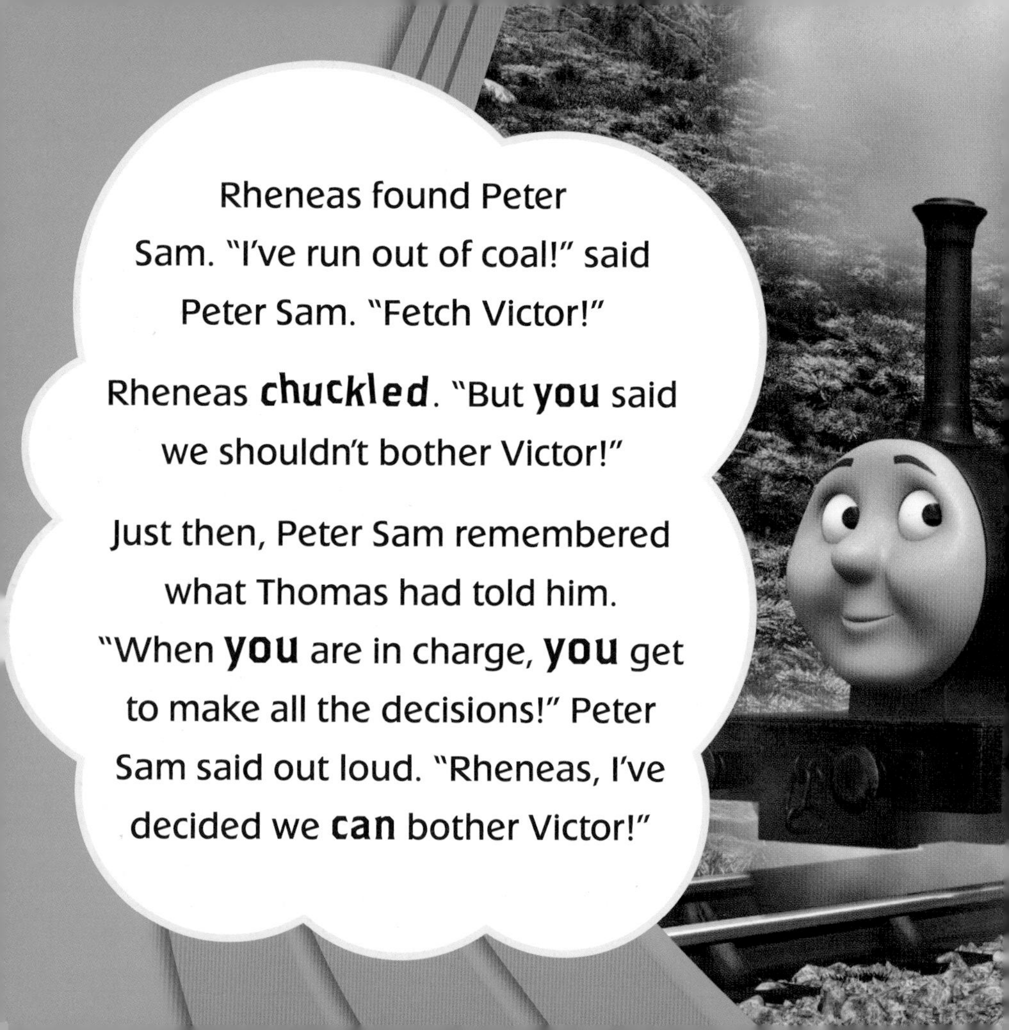

Rheneas found Peter Sam. "I've run out of coal!" said Peter Sam. "Fetch Victor!"

Rheneas **chuckled**. "But **you** said we shouldn't bother Victor!"

Just then, Peter Sam remembered what Thomas had told him. "When **you** are in charge, **you** get to make all the decisions!" Peter Sam said out loud. "Rheneas, I've decided we **can** bother Victor!"

PETER SAM
2
4

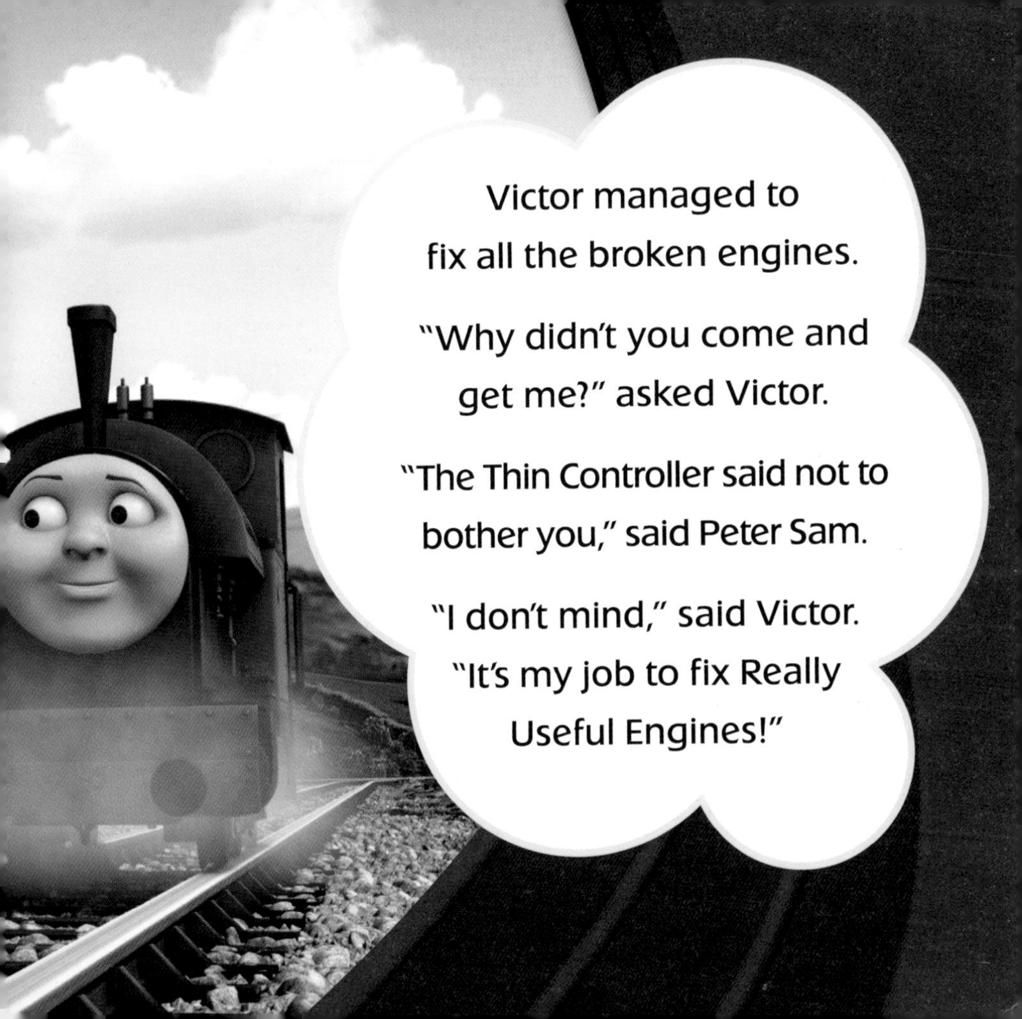

Victor managed to
fix all the broken engines.

"Why didn't you come and
get me?" asked Victor.

"The Thin Controller said not to
bother you," said Peter Sam.

"I don't mind," said Victor.
"It's my job to fix Really
Useful Engines!"

Later that day,
Thomas brought
The Thin Controller back
to the hills. "How was your day in
charge, Peter Sam?" he asked.

"**No bother** at all!" replied Peter
Sam. "Don't you agree, Victor?"

"I do," replied Victor. "It was
no bother at all!"

The End